To Ernie and Leo with lots of love.
You both know how to 'bee' a great friend.

– Mo O'Hara

To Ayame, Atsuko, and Yoko, your unwavering
friendship during my most challenging moments
means the world to me.

– Aya Kakeda

First published in 2024 by
Andersen Press Limited
20 Vauxhall Bridge Road, London SW1V 2SA, UK
Vijverlaan 48, 3062 HL Rotterdam, Nederland
www.andersenpress.co.uk

2 4 6 8 10 9 7 5 3 1

British Library Cataloguing in Publication Data available.

ISBN 978 1 83913 329 9

Printed and bound in Great Britain by Clays Ltd, Elcograf S.p.A.

Honey's Hive BEE A FRIEND

Mo O'Hara

ILLUSTRATED BY
Aya Kakeda

ANDERSEN PRESS

HONEY

BELLA

HEX

BEANIE

FRED

PETAL

CARL

MISS IVY

THE QUEEN

Chapter 1

Honey sat on a window ledge looking out at the garden of sunflowers below. The sun glinted off the windows of the high buildings around and warmed Honey's stripy fuzz. Her wonky antennae were twitching with excitement.

Sitting beside Honey were her friends: Hex, a tall clever honeybee who loved to design and build things; Beanie, a super-caring bee who loved looking after all the baby larvae in the hive; and Fred the flatfly (who was really a housefly, but as he lived in a block of flats, he called himself a flatfly. He liked to be precise about stuff.)

1

The friends were pleased to be spending some time with Honey, who seemed to be the busiest bee in the hive since she'd become the hive's scout bee. But none of them were prepared for what she was about to do next.

'Beeeee daaariiiiiiing!' she shouted as she bounced off the windowsill onto a leaf on the tree below and then somersaulted off the leaf like it was a diving board, before landing softly but clumsily on an open sunflower beneath them. 'Ummmmffff!'

Fred looked down at Honey and then over at Hex and Beanie. 'Does she do that a lot?'

They both nodded. 'Yup. Come on,' Beanie said, and they all flew to the sunflower.

'What did you just do?' Fred asked as he fluttered down next to her.

'Mnnnn mmmas mmying mme mee ma smwirl,' Honey mumbled, her face still firmly planted into the brown blossoms at the centre of the flower.

Beanie gently lifted up Honey's head and dusted her down.

'I was trying to be a squirrel,' Honey repeated, clearly this time. She sat up on the flower and shook her stripy fuzz to remove the extra pollen. But her bendy antennae flicked pollen onto the others instead. 'Ooops,' she said. 'Sorry.'

'You are lacking the counterbalance of a squirrel tail,' Hex said, tilting her head like she was doing sums inside it. 'Bees aren't really built to do tumbles. But we do have wings, so you could just use those.'

'Squirrels seem to have so much fun, though,' Honey said, standing up on the flower and brushing off her stripes. 'We need more fun. We're always so busy working. Busy bees.'

Let me just confirm what Honey said. Bees are indeed some of the busiest creatures in nature. In fact, a honeybee can beat her wings over 230 times per second. That's about 200 times faster than you can flap your hands. Go on and try. I'll wait . . . See. That's a lot of flapping. Right, let's get back to Honey and her friends.

'We do have fun sometimes,' Beanie said.

Hex giggled and nudged Beanie.

'Oooooffff. What was that for?' Beanie asked.

Hex winked. 'Talking of *fun*. We need to get back to the hive soon, right?' she whispered.

'Oh, yes,' Beanie said. 'We don't want to be late.'

'Late for what?' Honey asked as Hex and Beanie fidgeted and looked guiltily at each other.

'Ummmmm,' Hex said.

'The *thing*,' Fred said.

Hex nudged *him* now.

'Oooofff. Ummmm. That thing that is really not a very important thing but . . .'

'Miss Ivy said we had to be back for . . .' Hex paused.

'. . . Waggle dance practice,' Beanie said brightly.

Honey was sure she saw Fred and Hex sigh with relief. *They're up to something,* she thought.

'OK, I guess we should head back then,' Honey said. Then a cheeky smile spread across her face. 'Or . . . we could miss practice and do some more squirrel tumbles instead?'

Hex flitted over to one side of Honey, and Beanie to the other. They gently flew her off the sunflower and into the air.

'I love you, Honey, but I'm not getting a

detention from Miss Ivy because you're late for your own . . .' Hex started but stopped herself.

'My own *what*?'

'Waggle dance practice!!!' Beanie shouted.

'And if we're late we might miss the cake!' Fred added. 'Ooops. I wasn't supposed to mention that, was I? I just get a little overexcited when I know there is cake in the near future.'

'OK, bugs,' Honey flew back down to the flower and put all her arms on her hips. 'Spill the pollen. What's going on?'

Chapter 2

Just then Honey's no-nonsense big sister, Bella, swooped down and hovered above Honey and her friends.

'Don't spill any pollen. We need every speck of it back at the hive,' she ordered. Bella was a guard bee and took her job very seriously. 'I've come to check on you all. Miss Ivy was worried that you would be late for—'

'Waggle dance practice,' Beanie, Hex and Fred shouted together (not at all suspiciously).

Bella buzzed down and put an arm around Honey. 'Nice patch of sunflowers,' she commented, looking around. 'I'll send out the forager bees to them later.'

Just so you know, 'forager bees' are the bees whose job it is to go out and collect the pollen, nectar and water and bring it back into the hive. Every bee has their role in a hive and hard as it was for Honey to find hers for a while, she is now the hive's scout bee and very proud of it. Her job is to go and find the pollen, nectar and water in the first place.

'Hey, quiz time,' Bella said. 'Who remembers how to do a waggle dance for sunflowers?'

'Ooooh I LOVE quizzes,' Beanie squealed. She straightened up and did a very good daisy waggle dance.

'Nope,' Bella shook her antennae. 'That's for daisies.'

Fred, who liked to copy his bee friends, had a go at a waggle dance too.

'I think that's honeysuckle,' Hex said.

'It's the one that smelled the most like cake. That's why it stuck in my head,' Fred said.

Honey jumped into the centre of the sunflower. 'Well, if it's not this one then it should be,' and she started a very interesting and interpretive waggle dance that was a bit like Beanie's daisy dance but with everything much bigger. She ended it with a spinning squirrel move and a big 'TA DA!'

Her friends clapped at the performance but looked confused.

'Yup. You definitely need more waggle dance practice,' Bella said. 'Come on. Let's head back.'

But as soon as the insect friends approached the rooftop garden, Honey could sense that something strange was happening. And I don't mean sense as in the special way that bees can sense things with smell. This was more a general feeling like you might get if you were heading home with friends and then suddenly someone popped their head out of your front door and you heard them say, 'They're nearly here. Quick! Get ready.'

Because that is exactly what Honey saw and heard as she flew up to the entrance of the hive.

'What's going on?' Honey asked again.

Miss Ivy, Head of the Bee School, came to the door and motioned for her to go inside.

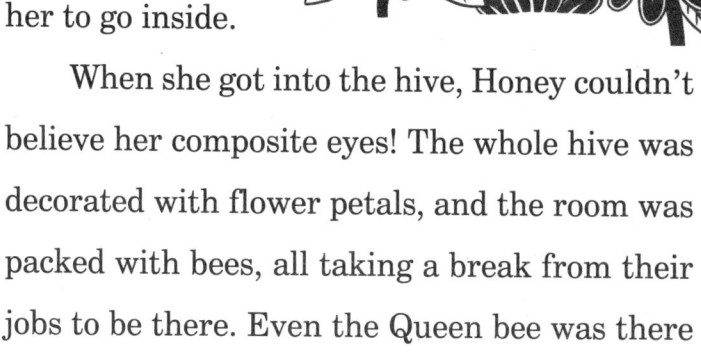

When she got into the hive, Honey couldn't believe her composite eyes! The whole hive was decorated with flower petals, and the room was packed with bees, all taking a break from their jobs to be there. Even the Queen bee was there and she buzzed forward when Honey flew in.

'Honey, please step up here,' she said.

'Hello, Your Majesty.' Honey attempted a curtsey to the Queen.

Then she whispered to Miss Ivy, 'Can you please tell me what's happening? Am I in trouble?'

Miss Ivy spoke loudly. 'Honey, as scout bee for this new hive, you have been—'

'I know,' Honey interrupted. 'I've been squirrel-jumping on the sunflowers, but I don't think it wasted any pollen, well, not much anyway, and it was a bit like training, and it was fun and how did you hear about it so fast? Am I in big trouble? Am I going to lose my worker bee job?' She said this in one breath.

She sucked in some air and was about to continue when Bella put her hand on Honey's shoulder. 'For once, you're not being told off. Just listen.'

Miss Ivy continued, 'As I was saying, as scout bee for this new hive you have been exemplary in your mission.'

Honey looked over at Hex as she had no idea what *exemplary* meant. Hex mouthed, *'That's really good.'* And gave her an antenna-up sign (which is like a bee equivalent of a human thumbs up. Obviously, bees have no thumbs.)

Honey smiled. 'Phew,' she said.

The Queen bee then spoke. 'So, it is our honour to present you with this petal pin as a reward for all your hard work for the hive.' And she waved Honey forward.

Honey was speechless. And it took A LOT for Honey to be speechless. Getting a petal pin was a massive honour for any bee. And it was happening to her. Bella nudged Honey to step forward.

'You need to actually receive the pin now,' Bella whispered.

'Oh yeah,' Honey mumbled. She stepped up and did another little curtsey. The Queen stuck the petal pin onto Honey's stripes, and everyone clapped.

'Three cheers for Honey!' Bella shouted.

Miss Ivy grinned. 'Thank you, everyone, you can now return to work. Busy as a bee, remember. We don't say that for nothing.'

'What about the cake?' Fred asked (slightly desperately).

'We will all have some honey cake after supper,' Miss Ivy assured him.

The other bees all headed back to their jobs. Beanie, Hex and Fred came up to congratulate Honey.

'I can't believe we managed to keep the secret,' Beanie said. 'I'm so bad at secrets.'

'I was the one who let slip about the cake,' Fred added.

'I knew something was up,' Honey said. 'But I never guessed it would be this. A petal pin! I'm so happy.'

'The Queen and Miss Ivy wanted to say thank you for all the great scouting you've been doing. You've found some really good food sources lately for everyone,' Beanie said.

'But . . .' Hex started to say something but stopped.

'But what?' Honey asked.

'But we've really missed you these last few weeks. It seems like you're always out scouting and you don't have as much time to hang out with us,' Hex continued. 'I know it's an important job, but we miss you.'

Honey's antennae tapped her friends'. 'I miss you guys too. It's just been really busy lately especially while Fred's been showing me the local area.'

'I like showing you around,' said Fred. 'I just wish there was more time for fun with friends too. And cake.'

'But I'm sure I'll have more time soon to—'

'Honey, are you going out for another scouting session this afternoon?' Miss Ivy called. 'Before cake?' she added, looking at Fred.

'I guess I gotta go,' Honey said.

'We need to get back to the larvae and the engineering block too,' Hex said.

'See you later,' Beanie called. But Honey had already flown off with Fred.

Chapter
3

'Let's head this way,' Honey said, turning right as they zoomed above the houses and tower blocks. 'I just have a gut feeling.'

'I always think it's best to follow your gut,' Fred agreed. 'Mine usually leads me to cake.'

As they buzzed over a field, Honey looked down and saw a familiar figure far below.

'Carl!' she called down to the lone carpenter bee, who was flying around some lavender. 'Look, it's my friend Carl,' she explained to Fred. 'Let's say hi.'

But as she and Fred flew down to see him, she noticed that Carl seemed to be moving very slowly. Like he was tired or sad, or both.

'Hi, Carl. Are you OK?'

'Oh, Honey, it's you. I'm not doing so well, actually, to tell the truth.' He shook his head sadly.

'What's wrong?' asked Honey.

'Well, there's no pollen or nectar left in this lavender and not much anywhere else around here either,' he said.

Honey remembered scouting that bit of lavender a few days before. The forager bees must have cleaned out all the pollen.

'I'm sorry, Carl,' she said. 'Oh, this is my friend, Fred. He's helping me scout out new food sources for the hive.'

'Hi,' said Fred. 'Actually, Honey's doing such a good job as scout bee, she just got a petal pin from the Queen!'

'I can tell she's doing a good job. For *her* hive,' Carl replied. 'But it's not leaving much pollen and nectar for the rest of us.'

'What do you mean, Carl?' Honey asked, fiddling with her new petal pin.

'Since your hive moved in, most of the pollen sources around here have been used up. There's not enough left for all the bees who were here before.'

'Are there many bees around here besides us?' Honey asked.

'There are lots of types of bees native to this area. And other pollinators too,' Carl said.

Sorry, I think I need to interrupt Carl here. Maybe I should fill you in on what a pollinator actually is. It sounds a bit like superhero, doesn't it? 'The Pollinator'.

Unfortunately, there are no bee action movie superheroes. But bees are pollinators, which means they move pollen from one flower to another. This is how flowers reproduce. Plants are, obviously, stuck in one place so can't meet up to exchange pollen, so they have to rely on some birds and mammals and mostly insects to carry the pollen around. Those creatures are called pollinators. Lots of insects are pollinators – moths, butterflies, beetles, wasps, flies and of course, bees. They all spread pollen from plant to plant and without them plants would die and fruit wouldn't grow. In fact, the planet wouldn't survive. So maybe they are superheroes after all!

Anyway, let's get back to Carl.

'There's just not enough pollen to go around now,' he said. 'Some of us lone bees and small groups can't compete with your growing hive.'

'Oh.' Honey stared at the fence, not wanting to look him in the eye. 'I'm so sorry.' She shuffled her wings. 'Maybe I can help show you where some food is too. I'm pretty good at finding it. Follow us,' she said, fluffing her wings and taking off. 'Come on!'

She flew Carl back to the sunflower patch she had been to earlier, but unfortunately the forager bees were already there gathering the pollen.

Honey, Fred and Carl landed on one bloom that had not been harvested yet and Carl gratefully gathered some pollen and drank some nectar, exhausted by the flight.

Bella flew over to Honey. 'I thought you were scouting somewhere else this afternoon. We have this patch covered for harvesting, Honey. No worries.'

'That's not what I'm worried about,' Honey said.

Carl buzzed over to Bella. 'Your hive has used up all the flowers here too?' he said. 'There are so *many* of you. Now that your hive is growing there isn't enough for the other bees who live around here.'

'I'm sorry,' Bella said, standing tall. 'And you are?'

'This is Carl.' Honey fluttered over next to him. 'He's the carpenter bee I met the night we found the new hive. Carl, this is my big sister Bella.'

'Pleased to meet you, Carl. And I'm sorry for your trouble but we had a really tough spring as a new hive and we have to build up our numbers and our food reserves.' Bella gave him a nod and flew up to join the forager bees. She needed to get them moving off towards home.

'Sorry, but we have to look out for our own,' she called back. 'I'm sure you'll find some flowers for yourself soon, Carl.' She smiled at Honey. 'I'll see you back at the hive for cake.'

Honey waved to her sister and looked back at Fred and Carl.

'*We have to look out for our own?*' Carl repeated. 'Well, your hive is certainly doing that.'

'Come on, Carl. She didn't mean to upset you. I'll help you take some sunflower pollen and nectar back to your nest.'

He shrugged and began to gather lots and lots of pollen with Honey. Fred looked at them and sighed.

Actually, fun bee fact, bees have nifty 'pollen sacs' which are just like pollen pockets on their back legs. I'm pretty sure if flies had those, Fred would end up filling them with bits of sugary sherbet. Back to the bees.

'Come on, Fred. We've got to get this pollen back with Carl.' Honey shook her antennae.

They all took off into the sky towards Carl's nest, laden down with scoops of pollen.

As they passed a clump of rose bushes in a garden, Honey noticed some small bees all buzzing about. But they weren't gathering pollen. They were cutting off bits of the roses' leaves.

'Hey, you bees!' Honey shouted down. 'You can't mess up those rose bushes like that!' She turned back to Fred and Carl. 'We have to stop them! Come on!' Honey zoomed down as a very confused-looking Carl and Fred followed.

Chapter
4

'OK, you leaf-wrecker bees,' Honey said and hovered overhead. *What is it that Bella says when she is warning people in her guard bee voice?* Honey thought to herself. *Oh yes.* 'Halt and explain yourselves!'

The smaller bees looked blankly at Honey as they continued snipping off bits of leaves from the rose bushes.

'Stop!' she said. She turned to Carl. 'Why aren't they stopping? Why are they damaging the rose bushes?'

'You might as well ask a honeybee not to buzz. These are leaf-cutter bees,' Carl said. 'Leaf cutting is what they do. And it doesn't hurt the rose bushes. The bees only take some of the leaves. They want the bushes to grow next season.'

'Oh,' Honey said. 'So, they aren't hurting the plants? Why do they do that then?'

'They live in nests like I do, instead of in a big hive like you,' Carl said. 'They are gathering bits of leaves for their nests. I'll introduce you.'

Carl fluttered down and landed by the busy bees. 'Hey there, folks!' he waved. 'I have some new neighbours to introduce you to.'

The leaf-cutter bees all gathered round as Honey and Fred flew down to the bush.

'Hi!' Honey said and waved with all her hands. 'Sorry about the shouting. I got a little carried away thinking you were going to rip up the whole rose bush. But then Carl explained that you are "leaf-ripper" bees . . .'

'Leaf-cutter bees,' Carl corrected.

'Right, sorry,' Honey smiled awkwardly. 'OK, let's buzz backwards and try that again. I'm Honey. Pleased to meet you, leaf-cutter bees.'

The leaf-cutter bees waved.

'Pleasure to meet you all,' said Fred. 'Really pretty roses.'

'It's a shame they don't have any pollen left on them,' one of the leaf-cutter bees piped up.

'Yes, we can get leaves for the nests but where are we going to get enough pollen from?' another added.

'See.' Carl looked at Honey, 'I told you. It's becoming a problem for lots of the bees in this area.'

Honey looked around the garden. She had definitely been here earlier in the week to scout and had reported back about these roses. The forager bees from her hive must have already harvested all the pollen. Honey felt a lump in her tummy. Not a hungry lump or an excited lump but a guilty lump. She didn't like the feeling at all.

'I'm sorry that my hive used up all the pollen from the roses,' Honey said, searching in her head for other flowers she could suggest to the leaf-cutter bees.

'I know where there are some big sunflowers. They might have some pollen left,' Honey suggested, trying to help.

'I know the way now. I can show them,' Carl said. 'But I think your forager bees have probably taken all that by now.'

'What other flowers do you like? I spotted some orchids on the windowsill of our block of flats,' Fred offered.

'I can't really drink from orchids. You need a longer tongue. Like bumblebees have,' Carl said. The leaf-cutter bees nodded. 'Honeybees are lucky because they can get pollen from lots of different flowers and they can fly further to get what they need. But the rest of us aren't so fortunate. We have specific tastes or needs.'

'Like what?' asked Honey. 'Let me help you.'

'Well, we love a bit of wisteria. Have you seen any of that?' one of the leaf-cutter bees butted in.

'Is that the dangling purple one?' Honey asked. 'Yeah, there was some of that in the church garden, beyond the pond and about three hedges away.'

The leaf-cutter bees looked excited. 'Come on, we'll take you,' Honey said.

The bees all followed Honey and Fred as they led them to the wisteria climbing the wall of the churchyard.

'Are we almost there?' one of the little bees gasped.

'It's just over here,' Honey pointed. 'Look.'

The leaf-cutter bees settled down gratefully on the wall around the wisteria plant.

'You look a bit tired,' Fred said to one of them. 'Have some nectar.' He pointed to the purple flower buds. 'It smells lovely and sweet.'

'Phew, yes that was a bit further from our nests than we would normally fly,' she said.

'We built our nests by the rose bushes so we could have food and leaves for building close by. Then all of a sudden, all the pollen was gone.'

Embarrassed, Honey looked down at the pin the Queen had given her. She took it off and slipped it under her hat.

The leaf-cutter bees set right to work, drinking nectar and gathering leaves and pollen to take home.

'We should head back to the hive,' Honey said. Fred nodded.

They said goodbye to Carl and the leaf-cutters and flew off over the wall and the churchyard towards the road.

'I feel terrible that we've been using up all the food around here,' said Honey.

'You weren't to know,' said Fred. 'You were just doing your job.' Then he stopped in his tracks. 'Do you smell that?'

Honey sniffed the air. Some car fumes, some smoke, some fresh-cut grass?

'What are you smelling?' she asked Fred.

'The cake? Can't you smell the cake?' he said, looking around for a bakery or an open kitchen window.

'No, that's honeysuckle.' Honey had finally caught the scent in the air. 'It smells like it's nearby. Come on.'

They followed the smell, past the churchyard and the shopping centre to the post office. There they found tall honeysuckle growing in the side garden.

'It smells so sweet,' Fred said, breathing in a deep sniff.

'Do you think if we brought back some of the pollen and nectar from here, we could show the hive that there are great food sources just a bit further away?'

'Good idea. I think we could carry a whole flower full of nectar between us if we flew carefully,' said Fred. And he sniffed the flower again.

'Great,' Honey said and they antennae-bumped. 'Let's do it.'

So they nibbled off a flower full of sweet-smelling nectar and lifted it up between them.

'Here we go,' Honey said.

But as they took off over the shopping centre and hedges, they began to notice a new smell. Honey and Fred sped up. They passed the sports field and headed for the hive in the rooftop garden as quickly as possible. Because they knew what this scent was and it certainly wasn't cake. It was the smell of danger.

Chapter 5

'Something's wrong,' Honey said as she sniffed the air. She looked around and, in the distance, she spotted them. 'Wasps!'

'WASPS??!!' Fred echoed. 'That is not good. They sting and bite and generally don't seem to like flies. Except as a snack for their larvae.'

'They don't like bees much either. Come on!' Honey sped up as fast as her wings would go.

Now, for those of you who don't know, wasps are about the same size as honeybees. But they are streamlined for speed whereas honeybees are made mostly for gathering pollen. Wasps are more like sports cars and honeybees are like cars with a big boot that can carry a lot of stuff.

In a race there would be no way a honeybee and a fly could outrun a wasp.

Plus this honeybee and fly were also carrying a honeysuckle flowerbud which slowed them down even more.

And the wasps were coming up fast.

'What are we going to do?' Fred asked desperately.

'I'm thinking,' Honey said. But no amazing ideas were hatching in her brain.

'Well, think faster or fly faster or both,' Fred said.

'OK,' Honey said. 'Well, we can't outfly them, so maybe we can trick them. Follow me.'

Honey and Fred flew lower along the high street. Past the newsagent's, bookshop, butcher's, until . . .

'In here,' Honey shouted, and she pulled Fred and the flower into the charity shop through the open door. They flew into a bunch of fake flowers in the window display. 'Don't move,' Honey whispered.

The two bugs sat silently in the fake flowers, keeping perfectly still.

The wasps zoomed past at first but then doubled back and sniffed the air outside the door of the shop. 'They can smell us,' Fred whispered.

'We need to go somewhere where there are lots of smells,' Honey said. 'That might confuse them.'

'Good idea, I think I know just the place,' Fred said and he pulled Honey up with the honeysuckle flower and they zoomed out of the shop. Honey looked over her shoulder to see the wasps dodging a rolled-up magazine that the shopkeeper was swatting at them with.

Fred led Honey down the street and around the corner to the bakery. Lots of sweet smells wafted out of the door.

'They won't be able to smell us in here,' Fred said, taking in a deep breath of lovely cake aromas.

The friends flew into the shop, ducked low to avoid the ceiling fan and then landed on the glass display case. Cakes, pies, and all kinds of tasty treats were displayed on the shelves below. Fred was drooling over the vanilla cupcakes and cream puffs but Honey was looking anxiously out of the door. Before long she spotted the wasps fly up to the front of the baker's shop and hover, looking a bit confused.

'We need to hide,' she said to Fred. 'They can't smell us as easily, but we are sticking out like a sore stinger sitting here.'

'Oh, I have an idea,' Fred said. He pulled

Honey over to the teacakes. They stuck the flower between two buns and landed on a teacake while the wasps buzzed past the cookie counter.

'OK, pretend to be a raisin,' Fred whispered.

'What?' Honey whispered back.

'Well, we are small and brownish, and so are raisins. Duck down and fold in your wings. Raisins definitely don't have wings,' Fred said.

Honey and Fred lay motionless on the bun, hardly daring to breathe.

The wasps flew past angrily and landed on the glass countertop by the till, searching and sniffing at the air. Just then the baker came out from the back of the shop with a tray of pies. He saw the wasps and shouted, 'Wasps! Get out, shoo!'

Grabbing a huge fly swatter from under the counter, he headed for the wasps. But as he passed the teacakes he looked down.

'And there's a fly on my buns!!!!!' he shouted and brought the swatter down hard on the teacake next to Honey and Fred, squashing several innocent raisins in the process.

'Let's get out of here,' Honey shouted, and grabbing Fred and the flower, she flew.

Luckily, the friends were closer to the door than the wasps. They cleared around the corner while the wasps had to swerve some close calls with the swatter before they made it out.

Fred and Honey buzzed along and could soon see the tower block a few buildings away. They were almost home. But not safe yet.

'We're nearly there. Do you think we can make it?' Fred asked.

'It's going to be close. Those wasps are fast,' Honey said, looking behind her. The friends sped up as quickly as they could. They flew up and onto the roof where Honey's hive was, but by now the wasps were catching up rapidly and buzzing right behind them. They weren't going to make it to the hive.

Suddenly, Honey heard a voice from one of the windowsills on the tower block.

'They're after the honeysuckle. Drop that

and you might get away,' a bumblebee shouted from a flowerpot.

Honey and Fred looked at each other. 'It's such a shame when we got it this far, but it's worth a try,' Honey said.

They dropped the honeysuckle flower over the edge of the building and it floated to the ground.

Chapter
6

As the flower fell, the wasps stopped, looked at Honey and Fred for a moment and then spun on their stingers and headed straight down after the flower.

The bumblebee was right. The wasps followed it and not them.

Fred and Honey watched as the wasps flew downwards, attracted by the strong sweet smell.

'Phew!' Honey said. 'Hey, thanks,' she shouted to the bumblebee.

The bumblebee flew up to the roof and hovered by Fred and Honey to watch. 'It's one of their favourite smells,' she said.

'Mine too,' said Fred. 'Thanks for the tip.'

'No problem,' she said. 'Hey, are you from the new hive?' she asked Honey.

'Yes. We wanted to bring the flower back to show my hive. I think we've been accidentally making things harder for the local bees by taking all the pollen,' Honey said. 'We didn't mean to, so I wanted to show my hive that we can get pollen and nectar from further away. Like that area with the honeysuckle.'

'Yeah, my nest is in the tree down by the school and I've noticed that there isn't as much pollen since you guys moved in. We're lucky that the school plants our favourite flowers in its field, but it's not been quite enough lately.

Those little humans at the school certainly seem to like bees though.'

'We used to have a human helper at our old hive,' Honey said.

'And they didn't swat you?' Fred asked. 'Most humans seem to swat at me.'

'Are they swatting at you when you land on their food?' Honey asked, tilting her head to the side and crossing her arms.

'Maybe . . .' Fred admitted.

'No, we used to let the human collect some of our honey and he tidied up the hive and brought us sweet stuff in the winter in return. He wore a ridiculous spaceman outfit though. Like that could stop us stinging him if we wanted to.' She shook her antennae.

'I don't think the little humans at the school know about your hive up here on the roof. Maybe if they knew, they could help you?'

'Thanks, but I think we need to help ourselves. I'm the scout bee for the hive, so it's up to me to convince everyone that we should share the flowers and that I should scout further away,' Honey said.

'Well, good luck with that. I've got my antennae crossed for you,' the bumblebee said. 'What are your names, by the way?'

'Oh my buzzness, I never remember to do that. I'm Honey and this is Fred,' Honey said.

'I'm Petal,' said the bumblebee.

'Excuse me, Petal. Do you have a long tongue?' Fred blurted out.

'Um . . . That's a very personal question to ask a bug you've just met,' Honey said, nudging Fred.

'Why do you ask?' Petal questioned.

'Well, another bee we know said that bumblebees can drink from orchids because they have long tongues. And I know a balcony on the other side of the building that has some orchids in bloom. Just saying . . . if you want a snack?' Fred offered. 'Plus, the lady who lives there normally bakes brownies on a Wednesday.' He smiled, dreaming of brownies.

'Yum,' Petal said.

'You guys go and check out the orchids and brownies. I'll get back to the hive,' Honey said.

Fred and Petal flew off and Honey tried to think of what she would say as she landed at the entrance of the hive. She already knew what Bella thought but maybe she could explain things to Miss Ivy or the Queen. Surely, they must appreciate that the hive needed to share with other bees.

Honey took a deep breath and headed inside.

But what she didn't see were the three wasps who had just flown up over the edge of the rooftop garden and were now staring at the hive.

One of them nodded to the other and started to laugh. 'A new hive? Up here? Why get nectar and food for ourselves when we can just steal what the bees have?' she said.

'Let's go back and get the others and then attack. These bees won't know what's hit them,' a second wasp replied.

'And just think, if the little honeybee and fly hadn't been carrying that flower here, we never would have found this place. It's our lucky day. Mwahha haa haa.'

'Hee hee hee,' the others laughed along.

If you are thinking that the wasps sound like evil insect villains, you would be right.

Chapter
7

The three wasps flew back down off the rooftop and away towards their nest.

But the plot thickens. (Which is just a storyteller way of saying that things are about to get even more complicated.)

What the wasps didn't know was that Hex had been on the roof of the hive, showing Beanie where they were planning to build an extension to house the Queen's new eggs. Beanie and Hex had ducked down out of sight when they saw the wasps approaching. Luckily the bees had excellent hearing and the wasps were buzzing pretty loudly so Hex and Beanie heard every word.

'Come on. We need to warn Bella and the other guard bees,' Hex said.

'And fast,' Beanie agreed.

Back inside the hive, Honey took a deep breath and went to see Miss Ivy.

'Ummmm. Would it be possible to speak to the Queen?' Honey asked. 'I have something important to discuss with her.'

'Of course, Honey. I'm sure she can spare some time,' Miss Ivy said, and she buzzed off down the hall, motioning for Honey to follow. 'Come along.'

Miss Ivy brought Honey to the throne room and ushered her inside to where the Queen was seated, surrounded by some of her guards.

'Your Majesty,' Honey said, dipping in a little curtsey.

'Ah, Honey. What can I do for you, dear? And where's your petal pin?'

'Oh, Your Majesty, I took it off. I don't feel I deserve it any more.'

'Why ever not?'

'Well, I found out today that what I've been doing has caused problems for lots of other bees. I wanted to see if you could help me fix it?'

'I'd like to try,' the Queen said. 'What appears to be the matter?'

'When I go out and scout for new food sources for our hive, the forager bees then collect them all and bring them back home.'

'Of course they do, that's their role in the hive.'

'But that means there isn't enough pollen for the other bees around here. There are lots of bee, like carpenter bees and leaf-cutter bees and bumblebees that were here way before we moved in. And some can't travel as far as we can. They're missing out on the nectar and pollen because we are using it all up,' Honey said. 'And it's all my fault.'

The queen paused. 'I'm very sorry to hear that.'

'So, what can we do about it?' Honey asked.

'I don't think we can do anything, and you mustn't blame yourself. I'm afraid this hive needs all the pollen it can get in order to grow and feed all the larvae that will hatch from the eggs I'm laying. Which reminds me . . . Please excuse me, dear.'

The Queen paused and waddled over to her chamber to lay a few dozen more eggs.

While the Queen is occupied laying her eggs I thought I should fill you in on how that whole laying thing works in a beehive. You see, when we talk about a queen bee laying eggs it's not the same as when we talk about, say, a chicken laying an egg. A chicken might lay one egg a day. A queen honeybee could lay up to 3,000 eggs a day. That's more than her whole bodyweight in eggs! Each day!

A chicken would have to lay sixty eggs a day to match her bodyweight in eggs. That would be one tired chicken. So generally, we can assume the queen of the hive is usually pretty exhausted from all that egg laying too.

Then Miss Ivy spoke. 'It's like Her Majesty said, Honey, we need all the pollen in order to become a strong hive. You are doing a fantastic job as our scout bee. Because of you, all the new larvae will be fed. The drones and the workers will eat and everyone will be happy.'

'But everyone *isn't* happy.' Honey stomped her legs. 'The local bees are very, very unhappy.'

'But we have to look after our own,' Miss Ivy said.

'That's what Bella said too,' replied Honey. 'But surely, we can look after each other. ALL of US. All the bees.'

Honey didn't wait for an answer. She flew off out of the throne room and bumped straight into Hex and Beanie, who were busy telling Bella about the wasps.

'Thank buzzness you saw them,' Bella said. 'Oh, Honey. There you are. Do you know what you and your fly friend have done? You've led wasps right to our door!' she shouted.

'Wasps? No, we lost them. They followed the honeysuckle—' Honey started to say.

'Well, they must have come back,' Beanie said. 'We were on the roof and we heard them laughing about following you and Fred and you leading them to the hive.'

'They're going to try and attack us,' Hex said.

'Why would you bring a whole flower full of sweet-smelling honeysuckle back to the hive, Honey? What were you thinking?' Bella said. 'You should have left it where it was, for the forager bees to collect from. That's their job.'

'I wanted to show the hive the great flowers that are a bit further away. Then we could save the closer flowers for the other bees who live around here and can't fly so far,' Honey said.

'Not that again.' Bella rolled her compound eyes and sighed. 'I thought I'd been clear.'

'We have to protect our hive first, Honey,' Hex added.

'Think of the larvae,' Beanie nodded.

'And now look what you've done,' Bella said. 'I don't know if we can defend against a massive wasp attack. I'll get the guard bees assembled. You two go and tell the Queen and Miss Ivy,' she said to Hex and Beanie. 'And Honey . . .'

'Don't worry, I'm going.' Honey flew past them and out of the door. 'I won't mess up anything else.'

Chapter 8

Honey flew off to the other side of the rooftop garden. 'All I was trying to do was help,' she said to herself and her antennae drooped sadly. 'Now I've brought wasps right to our door. They are better off without me there.'

Meanwhile, Bella had flown off to warn the other guard bees and make a plan whilst Hex and Beanie flew into the throne room and warned Miss Ivy.

'We have to remain calm,' Miss Ivy said. 'The worst thing we could do is all panic.' But she did look rather panicked as she said it.

Hex and Beanie flew out of the entrance of

64

the hive, looked around and tried their best not to panic too.

'It'll be fine. It'll be fine,' Beanie repeated, trying to calm herself down.

'But it's not fine, is it?' Hex said. 'And it's certainly not safe out here with the wasps coming. Where did Honey go? We need to find her.'

Fred zoomed up to the hive. 'Wasps? I thought we got rid of them,' he said as he fluttered down to the entrance, followed by a bumbling Petal.

'Watch out below!' Petal shouted as she flumped onto the entrance platform. 'Sorry about that. Didn't want to squash you. So, what were you saying about wasps? Have they come back?'

Hex and Beanie looked at Petal. 'Yes, and they are planning to attack our hive. Fred and Honey led them right to us with a flower full of nectar, and we overheard them plotting.'

'I really thought once the flower had been dropped, they'd just drink the nectar and fly away,' Petal said. 'That's really bad luck. I'm Petal, by the way. I met Honey and Fred earlier when they flew home.'

'Oh, are you one of the bees that Honey

was telling us about? The ones who need more nectar and pollen,' Beanie said.

'Yeah, I guess so. I'm a bumblebee. Our nest is down there by the school for little humans.' She pointed over the edge of the building. 'But yes, there are a lot of different types of bees around and we need to share some of the pollen you guys are using up. Bees should stick together. Honey was trying to help us all.'

'Yes, she's nice like that,' said Beanie.

'Fred told me about some orchids and Honey said she was going to speak to the Queen about your hive sharing more,' Petal said.

'And Honey helped the leaf-cutter bees to get some wisteria pollen, and Carl to get some sunflower pollen,' added Fred. 'She's been trying to make up for scouting out all the food in the first place. She really wants to help,' Fred said.

'It's a shame that no one can help us out like that now,' Hex said. 'I mean, to get ready for the wasp attack.'

'Hey, maybe we can. I can ask my sisters in my bumblebee nest,' Petal said. 'We could give you a hand.'

'And I can go and find the leaf-cutter bees and ask them,' Fred said.

'And we can ask Carl. I remember where his nest is,' Hex said.

'Maybe if we all work together, we can stop the wasps,' Beanie said. 'It's what Honey would want us to do.' They nodded.

'But we have to *find* Honey,' Hex, Beanie and Fred all said together.

Just then Bella interrupted. 'Where is Honey?' She strode out of the hive towards the group of insects. 'We need to find her. Where's she gone?'

'We don't know, but it won't be safe for long with the wasps coming,' Fred said.

'I'll go and look for her,' Bella said and paused. 'Actually, I might have an idea where to find her. I've instructed my guards on what to do for the attack. I'll be back as soon as I find that sister of mine.' She flew off, saluting the other bees.

'OK, we have our missions,' Fred said. 'We'll meet back here as soon as possible. This is quite exciting.' He jumped around and then looked seriously at the bees. 'Let's buzz this mission!' he said, punching the air. 'Oooooh, that could be my catchphrase.'

'Hex, what's a catchphrase?' Beanie asked as they flew off towards Carl's nest.

'Maybe it's a phrase you say when you're about to catch something?' Hex said. 'I don't know. Fred probably got it from watching TV through people's apartment windows again. Come on.'

Chapter 9

When Honey and her fellow bees all lived in their old hive, back in the railway garden, Honey had loved to fly to the top of the ivy-covered wall and sit and watch the world go by.

Now, she sat on the top of the ivy-covered wooden fencing by the shed in the rooftop garden. It was the most similar place she could find. She looked out at the buildings and the people and animals and insects all buzzing around in their own lives. She still felt that grumble in her tummy because she couldn't fix things for the other bees. All she had wanted was to get the hive to share and now she had led dangerous wasps right to their door and made everything worse.

'I thought I might find you here,' Honey heard Bella say as she flew down and landed on the fence next to her.

'I didn't think you wanted to talk to me,' Honey said.

'I'm sorry I yelled at you. It's not your fault, really. You were doing something you thought was going to be helpful. You are always trying to help out. And that's a good thing,' Bella said.

'But I led the wasps right to the hive. And now we can't protect ourselves. Let alone help anyone else.' Honey slumped down against an ivy stem.

'My little sister doesn't give up that easily. Come on. Let's get you to safety and I'll make those wasps regret they ever found our hive,' Bella said, pulling Honey to her feet.

They flew off across the rooftop garden and landed at the entrance to the hive just as the guard bees were all assembling to take on the wasps.

Honey could hear a buzzing. It was coming from below the roof edge. Something was on its way. The wasps! Were they here already?

She could see little figures flying over the top and heading towards them. Honey hunkered down to prepare but then, as the figures got closer, she spotted the familiar shapes of Hex

and Beanie. And they had Carl and some other carpenter bees with them. Behind them was Fred with a whole lot of little leaf-cutter bees and bringing up the rear was Petal and a big group of bumblebees. There was a whole bee squadron flying towards the hive.

Bella didn't know what to say. 'But why? How? Why are they here?'

Carl was the first to land. 'Because Honey needs our help. That's all we needed to know.

Hex and Beanie explained what had happened and we couldn't let your hive go up against the wasps alone. Besides, we carpenter bees and leaf-cutter bees have some ideas about how to protect your hive. We fortify our nests all the time to prevent attack.'

Lots of the other bees all began landing at the hive entrance too. 'Let's get to work, bees!' Carl said.

And the bees all started to buzz busily around the entrance. Some went off into the rooftop garden to collect bits of leaves or wood.

'What are they going to do?' Honey asked.

'Carl said that the carpenter bees are really good at using wood dust and chips to plug up holes in the hive. Sometimes wasps can use little holes to push through and invade the hive. If we plug up the holes, we'll be safer inside,' Hex said.

'That's a great idea,' Honey said.

'And the leaf-cutter bees said they pack tiny bits of leaves into the entrance of their nest to make it smaller,' Beanie said. 'So basically, the door is too small for most wasps to fit through. It's a pretty clever idea and they're going to show us how to do it.'

Petal landed on the entrance platform. 'Incoming!' she shouted as she bumbled to the floor. 'Phew,' she said, wiping her brows with her wing. 'That's a long way up. We don't normally all fly very far, but we wanted to help.'

'Thank you so much,' said Honey and she antennae-bumped Petal.

'Hey, we bumblebees are pretty chilled most of the time. "Live and let live" is pretty much our bumblebee code, but if we are under attack then watch out,' Petal said, wiggling her stinger.

'And you want to help us?' Bella asked. 'Why?'

'Because Honey wanted to help me and the other bees,' she said.

'Well, we could definitely use your help. Thank you. Fending off the wasps will be tough,' Bella said.

'And we bees have to stick together sometimes, right?' Petal said. 'Speaking of sticking, we like to spread sticky propolis on the entrance of our nest to protect us. It's like catching an intruder in sticky mud so we have time to knock them back and get them away.'

Hex nodded. 'That's a great idea. I'm on it. I'll get the propolis from the honey workers.'

Just so you know, propolis is a strange word for a very strange substance made as a by-product when bees make honey. It's a sticky gooey resin that is sometimes called 'bee glue'. Bees use to it seal up the hive to protect it from rain and sometimes from predators too. But it also has anti-bacterial and anti-fungal properties. So it helps keep infections and disease out of the hive. Pretty cool for some sticky gooey bee gunk.

The bees all got right to work fortifying the hive. Honeybees aren't the only busy bees, you know.

They sealed up the cracks, filled in the gaps, laid propolis sticky traps and shrunk down the entrance by packing it out like the other bees had shown them. They were as ready as they would ever be. And that's lucky because . . .

Honey heard the buzz of the wasps approaching.

'Right, all the rest of the honeybees, carpenter bees and leaf-cutter bees should get inside. Guard bees – you're with me,' Bella ordered.

'Fred, you'd better come inside with us,' Honey said. 'Come on. Let's check the Queen and make sure she's safe.'

'Good point. I'm with you,' Fred said.

They all piled into the hive behind the safety of the built-up leaf-stuffed door and the wood dust-stuffed walls but Honey still did not feel safe. The different bees all huddled inside as the noise of the wasps' approach got louder and louder.

Honey could hear Bella shouting to her fellow guard bees outside. 'Hold the line, guards! Hold the line!' as they stood together blocking the front door.

The wasp buzz got even louder. *They must be nearly here,* Honey thought.

Then Honey heard Petal shout out:

'Come on, girls, let's get ready to bumble!!!'

Chapter 10

Honey, Hex, Fred, Beanie, Carl and the other bees could all hear the commotion outside the hive.

Wasps were banging angrily against the door and walls, desperately trying to get in. Inside, Honey and her friends clung to each other in fear.

But what they couldn't see was that outside the hive, Bella, the guard bees and the newly arrived bumblebees were all doing a fantastic job at fending off the wasps. Whenever the wasps landed near the hive, the guard bees would push them off the ledge, or the bigger bumblebees would butt-bump them away with a powerful flick of their backsides. It was pretty impressive. But the wasps weren't giving up yet.

'We just need to get a few of us inside to steal the honey,' one wasp said.

'We can't get in this way. There are too many of them guarding the front,' another pointed out.

'Then we have to find a side way in,' the first wasp laughed. 'Come on.'

Back inside the hive, Miss Ivy and the Queen bee came out of the throne room and were more than a little surprised to see a hallway full of different kinds of bees.

'Oh, my,' the Queen said. 'Have we been invaded?'

'No, Your Majesty,' Honey said fluttering forward. 'All these other bees came to help us defend our hive from the wasp attack.'

The other bees all said hello and waved. The Queen did her many-armed queen wave back at them.

'Oh, I see,' she said to Honey. 'We thank you all,' she added to the other bees.

'You know if we are going to be in here for a while, we might all need a snack,' Fred suggested to Miss Ivy and then paused. 'I was thinking we could start on the honey cake that was meant for later?' He smiled hopefully.

'An excellent idea,' she replied. 'Everyone will need some food and energy after all their hard work. Come with me.'

As the other bees followed Miss Ivy and the Queen to get some honey cake and nectar, Honey started pacing back and forth in the hall.

'Aren't you going to get some cake?' Beanie asked.

'I don't think I can eat,' Honey said as she walked up and down the room.

'I don't think I've EVER felt I couldn't eat,' Fred said. 'That must be really bad.'

'It's OK, Honey,' Hex reassured her. 'It sounds like Bella and her guards and the bumblebees are holding off the wasps well.'

'Yes, but for how long? What if one gets in? What do we do then? We have to protect the Queen and the other bees,' Honey said. 'Oh, this is all my fault.'

'Hmmm,' Hex started pacing behind Honey, tilting her head in the way she always did when she was trying to figure out something complicated.

Beanie and Fred looked at each other. 'Might as well join them,' Fred said.

And the four bugs paced the floor of the hive, pondering what to do. Until Hex suddenly stopped.

'I've got it!!!' she shouted. The other bugs didn't stop quite in time and piled into her. 'Oooooof,' Beanie said, brushing off her fuzz as she stood up from the mound of bugs.

'What do you mean, Hex?' Honey asked as she stood and pulled Fred up onto his feet. 'What have you got?'

'I've got a brilliant idea!' she said. 'I remember learning something about the concept in bee school when we studied hive defence.'

'We studied hive defence?' Honey asked. 'I think I must have been daydreaming that morning.'

'Anyway, there is a method I remembered that uses the basic laws of thermodynamics to our advantage.' Hex bounced with excitement at her own idea.

'Could you say that in plain bee speak, please?' Beanie asked.

'Sorry. *Heat*. We use heat against the wasps,' Hex said.

'How do we do that?' Honey asked.

'It's called heat balling,' Hex said.

'Can honeybees shoot fireballs out of their stingers or something?' Fred asked.

'No, we can't shoot fireballs . . .' Beanie started.

'Shame. That would be very cool,' Fred shrugged.

'May I continue?' Hex asked and the others nodded.

'We bees can heat up our bodies so they are super-hot,' Hex said.

'Cool!' Fred said.

'No, *hot*,' said Hex. 'We can make them really hot!'

'So, we heat up our bodies and then what?' Beanie asked.

'Then we heat ball the wasps.' Hex smiled.

Everyone else looked blankly at her.

'And what does that do to the wasps?' Honey said.

'They can't handle the heat so they . . .' Hex started.

'Get out of the hive,' Honey finished her sentence. 'That's brilliant, Hex. Do you think it will work?'

'Well, it's worth a try,' said Hex.

'Bug team is on the case,' Honey said. They all antennae-bumped. 'We'll send those wasps packing.'

Sorry, I HAVE to interrupt again here because this is just too cool (or too hot) not to tell you about. So, I'm going to spill the pollen on heat balling. This is a genuine thing that some bees can do to protect themselves from wasps and hornets. Bees are very good at creating heat if they need to. For instance, if they need to keep the Queen warm in the winter. They can vibrate to generate heat and they can heat up their middles too. Well, at some point, some clever bee figured out how to use this to protect themselves from attack. You see, bees can withstand heat of up to 47 degrees Celsius (wasps can only stand it up to about 45 degrees). So, the bees surround the wasp in a heat ball and raise the temperature. The wasps overheat. The tricky bit is to keep the wasp surrounded. Now, let's get back to our bug friends.

Hex explained exactly what to do to Fred, Honey and Beanie.

'So I can go and get some cake now that we've got a plan if any wasps get in?' Fred asked.

Miss Ivy and the Queen and Carl all fluttered in at that exact moment, talking about lavender pollen.

'What do you mean you've got a plan if any wasps get in?' Miss Ivy said. 'We are completely safe in here, my dears.' She folded her arms securely and smiled at the Queen, who rustled her wings nervously.

'No wasps are getting in this hive,' she added, just as Beanie shouted:

'WASPS!'

Chapter
11

The group looked over and there, digging through a hole in the wall, was a huge angry-looking wasp.

Beanie squealed but something in Honey clicked. She looked at her friends and then over at the Queen and the others.

'We can do this, guys,' she said. 'Let's stick to the plan.'

The first wasp pulled herself out of the hole and stumbled to the ground.

'We'll take care of this wasp. You plug that hole!' she shouted to Carl.

'Are we really going to do this?' Beanie asked nervously as they stood tall and stared down at the menacing wasp.

'Yes, we are. Bee Code!' said Honey.

They all held hands and ran at the wasp together: Fred, Honey, Beanie and Hex.

'HEAT BALL!' Hex shouted as they barrelled into the enemy and knocked her off her feet.

Then they made an insect ring around her like a bee ball and started to heat up to their super-hot level.

'A heat ball?' Miss Ivy said, watching them in surprise. 'An excellent plan. Now, how do we plug this hole.'

'I can plug it with wax but it will take time,' Carl said. 'Another one could get in while I'm doing it.'

They looked around the room. 'There's nothing else big enough in the chamber to plug the hole with,' Miss Ivy said.

'Yes, there is,' the Queen suddenly interrupted.

'ME!'

'Your Majesty?' Miss Ivy said with surprise.

But just then they all heard rustling outside, behind the hole. 'Quick, another one is trying to get in,' Carl said urgently.

'There's nothing for it then,' said the Queen and she waddled towards the hole in the wall, turned herself around and planted her bottom (stinger first) into the hole.

The bees all heard a muffled 'Oooouuch' from the other side. 'Well, that ought to send them back out again,' the Queen said.

'I'll go and grab some more carpenter bees and get that hole filled from the outside,' Carl said and he flew off with some of his friends towards the entrance.

'Are you all right, Your Majesty?' Miss Ivy asked.

'Perfectly fine if a bit uncomfortable,' the Queen said. 'Now go and help our young friends in their . . . what was it again?'

'A heat ball, ma'am,' Miss Ivy answered.

While all this was going on Honey, Beanie, Hex and Fred had been rolling around the room in a big ball of bugs surrounding the wasp and getting hotter and hotter and hotter.

'Wooooah!' They careered to the left of the room.

'Wooooah!' They rolled to the right.

The wasp was getting drowsy from the heat. 'Who knew honeybees had such hot hives,' the wasp mumbled.

'It's working,' Honey said. 'Keep going, guys.'

'I don't think I can . . .' Fred said and then his fly eyes glazed over. 'I see a big lemon cream pie. Let's head for the pie.'

'Oh no, the heat. It's getting to Fred too. He's seeing things,' Hex said. 'He can't take this, we'll have to drop him out of the heat ball or he could get really sick.'

'But if we do that, we'll break the circle and the wasp will get away,' Beanie said.

'I want to help,' said Fred. 'I just also really want the lemon cream pie.'

'Don't worry, I can step in,' Miss Ivy shouted. She jumped onto the rolling ball of bees and unclasped Fred from Honey and Hex. Fred tumbled to the floor as the bee ball rolled on.

'Thank you, Fred, but you can take a rest now,' Miss Ivy said.

Miss Ivy heated up to make the ball even hotter with four bees on the job.

'I don't feel so good,' the wasp mumbled. 'I think I might be sick.'

'Let's get her out of here,' Honey said. 'I have an idea. Hex, Beanie, let's try a squirrel tumble heat ball?'

'I have absolutely no idea what you mean but I'll roll with it,' Miss Ivy said. 'I'll literally roll with it.'

Honey pulled back from the ball and ducked down, bouncing them off the ground and sending them towards the entrance like a spinning, tumbling rubber ball of bees. Honey steered them with bounces. Right, then left, then out the front. They burst out of the entrance hatch past the guard and bumblebees and the remaining wasps.

Honey, Beanie, Hex and Miss Ivy all shouted as they bounced into the air out of the hive.

'AAAAAAAAhhhhhhhh!'

Chapter 12

'Release now!' Honey shouted and they all unclasped hands and dropped the wasp onto the plants below.

The wasp looked green. (And wasps really don't look green except when they feel really, really yucky.)

She fell to the ground and landed in a plant pot by the hive. Her head was spinning and her wings were squashed and her antennae were twisted and she felt really, really hot.

Her fellow wasp, who had been trying to break in with her, flew down to help.

'I just got stung on my face trying to crawl through the hole after you.' She sounded a bit like you would sound if you spoke while trying to hold your nose closed at the same time.

Go on, try it. Hold your nose and say something. I'll wait . . . See what I mean?

The first wasp said, 'You were lucky. I don't know what happened in there, but I feel awful, and I didn't get any honey. Whose idea was it to attack this hive anyway?'

'Yours!!!' the second wasp said.

'Well, don't listen to me. It was clearly a bad idea.' The wasp shook her head. 'Let's get the rest of the wasps and clear off before those bees do that heat ball thing again. Come on.'

'I'm never coming back here,' the other wasp agreed. 'And the rest of the gang have been knocked around out here and bumped about by bumblebee butts. Worst hive attack ever!'

'I don't ever want to look at another beehive. And this one is spinning a bit. Or is that my head?' the first wasp mumbled.

'Come on. Let's get you somewhere in the shade to cool off,' the second wasp said as they took off.

They shouted to the remaining wasps as they flew past:

'Abandon the attack!

Let's get out of here.'

The bumblebees and guard bees cheered as all the wasps took flight.

'That's right. And don't come back!' Bella shouted after them.

'Boom,' Petal said, tapping antennae with Bella. 'A bit of a bumble in the jungle. We saw them off! Woo hoo!'

The bees all fluttered down to the hive entrance platform to rest.

But Honey, Beanie and Hex were racing back inside to check on Fred.

'Excuse me. I need to get through,' Honey buzzed as she pushed through the crowd of bees into the hallway chamber to find him.

'Fred!' she called. 'Fred! Are you OK?'

'Turn up the air conditioning, ladies,' the Queen said, and the worker bees who were sitting on the floor around Fred all sped up their wings so that they blew like tiny fans on him and cooled him down.

Honey looked over at Fred relaxing on the floor with a refreshing cup of nectar in his hand.

Hex and Beanie raced in behind Honey. 'Phew. He looks much better,' Beanie said.

'Yes, I remembered that my attendants sometimes cool me down in the summer with their own wing fans so I thought they could do that for your fly friend,' the Queen said.

This is actually what happens in a warm hive in summer. Forager bees not only collect pollen and nectar, they also collect water and some of the water is used to cool the hive and the Queen. The way it works is some of the bees spit the water out and other bees fan that cool water so that it evaporates and lowers the temperature of the hive. It works in much the same way as an air conditioner in a building. Except for the spitting part obviously. You might get asked to leave a building if you started spitting out water and flapping around fanning the water away. That is exactly what the Queen's assistants were doing though and it was working.

'Thank you, Your Majesty,' Honey said to the Queen and then asked Fred, 'Are you OK?'

'I'm fine,' Fred said. 'Bit disappointed that the lemon cream pie wasn't real but I'm told there is plenty more honey cake, so that's OK.' He smiled.

Just then Miss Ivy came into the room. 'Your Majesty, the wasps have been defeated,' she said with obvious relief.

All the bees in the hive gave out a huge cheer.

'What a wonderful example of the Bee Code,' continued the head teacher.

'The Bee Code?' said one of the leaf-cutter bees.

Miss Ivy explained.

'A Bee must . . .
Bee loyal, bee strong.
You must always get along.
Bee considerate, bee kind.
Work hard and you'll find
Your place in the hive.
You'll help it survive.
Together, you see,
You can be your best bee.'

Petal the bumblebee nodded. 'We have a bee bonding song that is a lot like that. But it's got a better groove.'

Honey smiled at Petal and they tapped antennae.

'What we did today,' Miss Ivy continued, 'the carpenter bees and leaf-cutter bees securing our hive, the guard bees fighting for our survival, Her Majesty plugging the hole and you young bees having the clever idea of using a heat ball – all showed how together we are stronger. And we helped the hive survive.'

Honey put four hands on her hips. 'It was a real team effort,' she said, 'and the heat balling was Hex's brilliant idea.'

'Well, I'm glad someone was paying attention in hive defence class,' said Miss Ivy.

Honey looked over at Hex and giggled.

Fred finished his cup of nectar. 'Yes, you bees do make a pretty good team,' he said.

'And add a fantastic flatfly into the mix and you can't go wrong,' Honey added. 'We do make a strong team.'

'That's good,' the Queen said, wiggling her backside, 'because I might need a strong team to pull me out of here. I do believe one is stuck.'

Chapter
13

'We'll help,' Honey said. She and her friends raced over, grabbing one of the Queen's arms each and pulling.

'HEAVE!!!!' Honey shouted as they yanked together.

'Still not moving,' Hex said. 'Try and wiggle and pull at the same time, Your Majesty.'

'One shall wiggle,' the Queen said.

'One! Two! Three! And heave,' Honey shouted as they pulled again.

The Queen's bottom unstuck from the hive wall with a satisfying 'POP!' and all the other bees fell backwards in a heap on the floor.

POP!

'Phew,' Hex said.

'Exactly,' said the Queen. 'Phew. One is relieved to be free at last. Now, did I hear a mention of honey cake?' She smiled. 'One is quite peckish after all that exertion.'

Honey looked over at Hex for a translation. 'She's super hungry from all that work,' Hex whispered to Honey.

'Me too!' Honey said.

'Then . . . let them eat cake,' announced the Queen.

So, the bumblebees, leaf-cutter bees and carpenter bees all joined Honey's hive to celebrate warding off the wasps.

Carl took a sip of nectar and then spoke up, 'Must be said, I'm normally a bit of a loner, but I saw today how special it is and what you can achieve if you work together.'

'To working together,' Miss Ivy said and raised her cup of nectar too.

Petal and Bella clinked cups of nectar. 'To new friends,' they both said.

'What was it that you said this morning when you jumped off the windowsill trying to be a squirrel?' Fred asked Honey.

'Mmmmmfff mffffmm meeeemmm?' Honey mumbled into her arm.

'No, I mean not what it sounded like. What did you actually shout as you jumped?'

Honey shouted and threw in a little squirrel tumble for good measure:

'Beeeee daaariiiiiiing!'

'Oooooof,' she said as she rolled up and bumped into one of the bumblebees. 'Sorry. Think I said that too.'

'That's it. Be daring,' said Fred. 'I think that's kind of what we all were today. Daring.'

'The bumblebees were definitely daring. Bumping all those wasps away from the front of the hive,' Bella said.

'And the carpenter bees were daring when they went out in the middle of the battle to seal up the hole in the wall from the outside,' Beanie said.

'And the Queen was pretty daring plugging the hole from the inside too,' Honey said.

'And the leaf-cutter bees were really clever and daring in the way they fortified the entrance with the leaves. Good engineering principles there.' Hex nodded.

'Honey, you and your friends were super-daring doing that heat ball thing. Wow,' said Petal.

Honey blushed. It's kind of hard to tell when a bee blushes with all the stripes and stuff, but if you looked very closely there was a faint hint of pink glow in her cheeks, under the black and yellow stripes of course.

Honey fluttered forward. 'So, if we can be that daring when we *need* to be maybe, we can be daring when we *want* to be as well?'

'What do you mean, Honey?' Miss Ivy asked.

'Maybe we honeybees could dare to share the pollen and nectar with all the other bee friends we've just made.'

'We didn't expect you to pay us back,' Carl said.

'No, I know. You dared to share your time and your knowledge to help us,' Honey said. 'No strings attached. Now we could dare to share our pollen. Not because we have to but because it's the right thing to do,' she added.

'We should,' said Bella.

'Definitely,' said Hex.

'Of course,' said Beanie.

'You are very wise for someone so young, Honey,' the Queen said. 'And you are absolutely right.'

Miss Ivy tapped antennae with Carl and Petal. 'We'll make a plan tomorrow to scout further away and look for flowers that the other bees can't use as much.'

'Buzz buzz hooray!' 'Buzz buzz hooray!' 'Buzz buzz hooray!'

The bees all cheered.

Honey took the flower pin out from under her hat and pinned it to the front entrance of the hive.

'I think we all deserve this today,' she said.

Chapter
14

It was late afternoon by the time the party broke up and the visiting bees all headed back to their nests. The leaf-cutters headed for their rose garden; Carl and the carpenter bees headed for the fence by the field; and the bumblebees got themselves ready for the flight down to the tree in the schoolyard right by Honey's building.

Petal sighed. 'I'm exhausted,' she said. 'That's more flying than we ever do in a day, isn't it, girls?'

The other bumblebees nodded and yawned.

'I wish there was an easy way down instead of flying,' Petal said.

Honey, Hex, Beanie and Fred shared a look. 'The lift,' they said together.

Just then they all heard a *ping* as the lift door opened onto the roof garden.

'Did we do that?' Beanie asked.

'No. Someone must have come up in the lift,' Fred said.

A couple of small humans and an older woman with a cardboard box stepped out.

'Look over there,' one of the small humans shouted and started to run. 'There they are. I told you I saw a whole swarm of bumblebees fly up here.'

'Don't run, Mia,' the older woman said. 'You'll scare the bees.'

'Why would the bees be scared of me, Abuela? There are lots of them and only a couple of us,' she said.

'I like this small human,' Honey said to Petal. 'Hey, are they from the school where you live?'

'Yup. They are sweet. The bigger human is the one who planted nice flowers for us in the schoolyard,' Petal said.

The lady stepped forward slowly with the box. 'OK, lovely bumblebees, you must be tired from all that flying. Do you want to have a little rest in the box and we'll take you home?'

'It's like the bumblebees ordered a cardboard taxi to take them home,' Fred smiled.

'I don't know what a taxi is but if it's comfortable then I'm all in. Come on, girls. Let's hitch a lift home,' Petal said and she fluttered sleepily towards the box to settle in. The other bumblebees followed.

'I think you've got them all, Abuela,' the little human said.

Then the grandmother put the lid on the box. But before she lifted it off the ground, she came over to look more closely at the hive.

Honey, Beanie, Hex and Fred all stood perfectly still on the platform outside the entrance.

'Well, look at that. Honeybees.' The lady rubbed her glasses and looked again. 'And a fly?'

'Hmmmm?' she mumbled and then gently reached over and lifted the roof off one corner of the hive.

'I didn't know that the roof did that?' Honey said.

'Me neither,' Hex said. 'But it makes sense. Our old hive had a lid that came off so the human could come and take some honey sometimes.'

'There are honeybees in the hive. Looks like lots of them. And what nicely shaped honeycomb too. Wow. Well, what do you know?' the lady said and smiled. 'There haven't been bees here for years. Not since your papa was a boy.'

She looked around the garden. 'Well, if there are this many more bees, we'd better get busy planting some more flowers for them all.

We'll get the rest of the kids in your class to help. We could make it a project.'

'But will the bees hurt us?' the other little human piped up.

'Oh no. You just have to be a bit gentle and give them space. Maybe we can plant some big bold lovely flowers for them.'

'Yellow class could help plant some,' one of the little humans said.

'Let's check with your teacher tomorrow but for now we have to get our sleepy bumblebees home,' the lady said and she ruffled the little human's hair.

'Bye bye, Petal!' Honey shouted as the humans took the box to the lift.

But all they could hear were the happy sounds of buzzy bee snores from inside the box.

The humans walked over to the lift and it gently pinged as the doors closed.

'Well, it looks like we might be human keepers again,' Honey said.

'Human keepers?' Fred asked.

'The humans who take the honey call themselves beekeepers, but that's just silly, we're the ones looking after *them* really,' Honey said.

Hex and Beanie nodded.

'The little ones are really sweet,' Beanie said.

'I like the old human. She appreciated my well-made honeycomb,' Hex added.

'Let's go tell the others,' Beanie said.

'Wait a buzz,' Honey said. 'I just wanted to say sorry.'

'What, for the wasps? I led them here too,' Fred said.

'No, to Beanie and Hex for not spending more time with them.'

'I think we'll all have more to do now that we have humans to keep,' Hex said.

'But we'll all make time for each other,' Beanie added.

'We make a pretty good team,' Fred said.

'We were three bees in a pod,' said Hex. 'But now we're . . .' She paused and thought.

'Four bugs in a hug,' Beanie said and grabbed them all in a big squishy bug hug.

'Oh my buzzness, that's cheesy,' Honey said, wriggling in the hug.

'What can I say? I'm a sentimental bee,' Beanie said and squeezed tighter.

'You're not going to heat up again or anything, right?' Fred mumbled from inside the hug. 'I've had enough heat for one day.'

And they all laughed.

'I hope we never have to do that again,' Beanie said. 'That was scary.'

'But kind of exciting too,' Honey said. 'And did you see my squirrel tumble? I nearly nailed it, I think. Maybe I just need a bit more practice.'

Honey stood up on the edge of the hive and looked at the springy patch of grass below.

Hex looked over at Fred and Beanie. 'You know what she's going to do, right?'

'Yup.' Beanie nodded.

Fred grabbed arms with Hex and Beanie and led them to the edge next to Honey.

'One . . . Two . . . Three . . .' he counted down.

The four bugs all smiled and leaped into the air together. 'Beeeee daaariiiiiiing!' they yelled into the evening sky as they all attempted a dynamic squirrel tumble off the ledge.

Did they ever master the squirrel tumble? Did they actually just end up in a crumpled pile of bugs on the grass, giggling? Did the little humans come back to help plant some lovely new flowers for the bees?

Well, I could tell you. Or I could leave you in suspense until the next time we see Honey and her friends.

You won't bee-lieve what they get up to next!

Build a bee hotel

Cut some strips from a cardboard box and roll them up

Take a tin can and place the rolled-up cardboard in lengthways. Add some small sticks from a garden and park

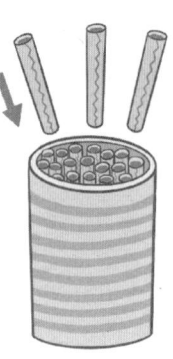

Tie some string around the can and hang it up on its side in a bush

Plant a bee-friendly garden or window box

- Pick lots of different types of native flowers. Native bees like native flowers.

- Create a 'bee corridor'. You can do this by planting rows of wildflowers to connect gardens. Why not get your school or neighbours involved too?

- Let part of your school grounds or home garden grow wild with wildflowers.

Create a bee pond

It doesn't have to be big. Just an old aluminium or plastic tray filled with pebbles (so the bees have somewhere to land), and water. Place it outside to give bees a place to rest and drink.

And bees don't mind dirty water either. They love drinking from the trays below flowerpots.

Please don't swat

Bees can be curious but they rarely sting. Don't go close to a nest or hive, but if you see a bee flying around, don't wave her away, she might get scared. Just let the bees be.

Why help bees now?

Bees pollinate over ninety-five per cent of our main food crops worldwide. UK bees have lost ninety-seven per cent of their wildflower habitat in the last sixty years. We need to stop using pesticides that kill the bees and pollute the land. Let's rewild bee habitats so bees have places to live and respect bees as a super-important part of the natural ecosystem. One person, one class or one neighbourhood can make a big difference to bees.